LOVE POEMS

11/01/24

Keith Keenan

artnewyork.com

For Dear Lanfen, I dedicate this book

CONTENTS

Title Page

Copyright

Dedication

EROS   1

Heat   2

Silk   3

Starting Over   4

Rush   5

Yellow Slippers   6

Wretched   7

Love Fits   8

Depression   9

Endure   10

Outlawed   12

If   13

Haiku for Lanfen   14

Lanfen   15

Nature   16

Predestined   17

Spring   18

Seed   19

Memory   20

Echo   21

Berries   22

LiZA   23

Sunday   24

Inside the Bubble With Liza   25

Dinner   26

Dead man   27

Liza Speaks   28

Peak Experience   29

Abortions   30

Banshee   31

Pause   32

Revenge   34

About The Author   37

EROS

HEAT

We ran the barren shore as if August
had put us there, two brush marks
in the noonday light, yelling
over the loud ovations of the waves,
the spray sparking like fireflies,
the sun hot & intermittent on our faces,
our bare feet on the burning sand,
turning the dunes into a sanctuary
where, under the cottonwoods,
we tumbled like children onto grass
until everything was green. I still feel
the grass blades on my cheek, your eyes
on me & in that final madness,
the mad intrusion of the hairy bee.

SILK

When you, my love, are metaphor, my whole
creative life like starlight the dazzle on my brain,

I am newly coined, watching you exit
showers or baths, your breasts delightful as babies,

your body looking like Sunday, your consent
orbiting mine, bringing us closer

like bees in a hive or strings in a knot.
How much you please without trying like silk,

and when the night stalls and takes on your shape,
radiant as any resurrection, you surround my existence,

overwhelming my senses with animal insistence,
driving me on like rapids with so many words

and so much surrender that I, unable to hold back,
fall to pieces on the whiteness of your body

before morning geysers up with birds and clouds,
and I touch your sunlit face to be warm forever.

STARTING OVER

When whispers fall through the cracks
into young boys' ears, and everyone caresses,
sucks and gasps, smelling of sweat and heat.
When dawns open like crisp apples,
and sunlight scatters over unmade
beds, lovers' part. When life refuses
to stop, and babies, healthy as trout,
come from every direction under a toiling sun
and taste the salt of life, I discover
I exist as if death is only an idea
with a girl, essential as water and bread,
who dresses in sunlight one day at a time.

RUSH

When we touch, your nerves are a million eyes
watching my fingers pull from you whispers
and sighs; you are why the night stalls,
a birth that will never cease, an opening
that will never close, a continuous sunrise
where life swells into being in your body
of consuming love always giving,
and what you give you set free and listening
are never closed for in you everything
is kept: your consent orbiting mine
and your depths below which there is nothing
and above which there is only me
with my many hands and my frenzied desire
no longer disguised by routines.

YELLOW SLIPPERS

Laughter mingles with children's voices as I leave the Low Road,
lonely as secrets, the butt of a thousand rumors, as evening,

flowering on wet streets, follows me down to the river
that shines like ink exhaling what light is left as I sadly reflect.

When the priest said dance that night in Saint Albans' gym,
we stepped on each other's feet but learned to touch.

God gave me two choices when I only needed one.
Take your partners, please, and I took you instead of Mona Pop.

We took lessons loving each other, you a girl with small breasts,
a determined girl who followed me around until I followed you
        into bed.

The priest said marry, but you were a cat leaping onto the moon
and I, just a boy, with too many hands and no ears.

You had to be more than unnoticed, you said, yet refused
to give in on so many things. Peace is like that, I said,

but I didn't understand how close to heaven I came
until you walked into shadows, waved quickly, and deserted me.

You left behind your yellow slippers and our chalked heart
on the cricket field wall. Now I want to break

bread with God and ask Him straight up, "Why?"
and in case He doesn't know, tell Him, "This is hell."

WRETCHED

After your no, I died. The rest of my death
I spend staring out the window,

as Autumn turns, and frost glitters
like cut apples in the morning light,

and the delicate butterfly flowers
and snapdragons call it a day.

My backyard is a remorseful funeral,
and I am lost in a dirge of my own making,

watching my wretched ghost, leaving
its station, slouch from room to room.

Now I'm learning to take off my pants
slowly and walk to your side of the bed

as if I have somewhere to go. Months
go by before I gradually come back to life,

so seeing you now in your cotton dress,
radiant as apples, is more than I can take

and though nothing is said, I would die
to touch you again, pulling from you

whispers and sighs, listening to the rush
of your breath, the red bees swarming

about your heart, as you gang up on my senses,
submissive as water, persistent as rivers,

with panther eyes and animal insistence,
wild as the night sky and like the day a parade of births.

LOVE FITS

I'm searching inside Sunday for clues
of your whereabouts from the music
you make by breathing, hurrying to you
before all directions are used-up,

following the minutes like tiny crumbs,
watching you chase dark from corners,
and decipher my chaos, turning each day
into a keyhole to the rest, teaching me

I need exceptional women to exist
like you, who calms the child whimpering
like a flame, who is the love that was
always elsewhere until I saw
honey bees swarming about you.

You turned from gardens and children,
came running past stars and crosses,
undiscovered, awaiting my astonishment,
my mind of snakes engendering words
to bed you down and chase the doves
from the white nests of your body.

Today you are my heaven and I your god,
knowing love fits and inhabits everything
with a future like air and water or the harvest
from the seed or the poems I lift from your body
to make honey in the hive of your mind.

DEPRESSION

When birds shut their wings, and the vacant sky
eludes them, and the day leaves me stalled
in empty rooms, I imagine a destiny
of rain, a cupboard of tins, women
with abusive men, and days that never arrive
and never end. When all doors slam tight,
and a blaze of forsythia turns to ashes,
and I see my demise as an advantage,
I know the ocean with its submerged
eternities, the sky with its endless prison,
and I listen to my wishes scratch at the window
as I shout your name: Jane, Jane, Jane, and wait
for your door to open, for you to walk-through
with your freckled face looking so much like you.

ENDURE

I hear it in whispers and sighs,
frantic positioning,
the skilled bee sucking
the stamen all over,
in desire breaking its chains,
consents that peak
in a rush like rapids.

I hear it in spring,
in births so much like me,
in you juicing me
with so many hands
and so many words,
submissive as water,
persistent as rivers.

I hear it in me,
in concupiscent schemes,
in dramas I binge on,
in days that sting or smile,
riding them down
to autumn and seed,
taking you with me.

I hear it in prayers,
in chants and rituals,
that ward off oblivion
and give me the power
to step out of my body
into the make-believe
world and live.

I hear it in the night
outside of my window, the lights,
like colored confetti,
scattered over us so close

we plan to stay here for now,
knowing there's so little time
to be kind to each other.

OUTLAWED

I cannot remember if I loved you.
Perhaps I lied when I said I did,

but you are gone, and it seems now
your life was told to me in my sleep.

I want to tell you I'm sorry,
but that will never be except in a dream.

There's no sense to the lies, I tell myself;
so I drop the pretense,

knowing I can't step out of my body
into the make-believe world and see you again.

Without you, my hands are lonely,
the dazzle has gone from the day,

and the hum of each moment —
my brain's continuous chatter

tells me I'm truly alone, yet everything
I touch reminds me of you:

the empty vases and unmade bed
that reveal my love is strongest without you.

You are like a forecast of good weather
that never arrives,

yet I wait at your exit restless and outlawed
in a space that remembers you're gone.

IF

If I could
awaken you,
my love,
and chase
oblivion away,
I would answer
your prayer
and speak
like a fool
to the bees
bestowing
existence
and to the stones
that come
to my hands
as reminders
and to the sun
that no longer
finds you,
but what can
I really say?
Today
I am cut in two,
discovering in you
futures
like empty rooms
and unexplained exits,
and in myself
a desire
to join you,
and a rope
hanging from a sky
I want to climb to.

HAIKU FOR LANFEN

Steamed sea bass and rice
and a cup of oolong tea
with the one I love.

LANFEN
My love

I see your name
travel out of every bud

with the news of your return
in a white dress

looking like your name
I write on top of my poem

after sunlight breaks
the fast of white wisteria

sweetness in the air
I share with you asking

will you come will you
before it's too late

you have
nothing to lose

so come with me now
the day will come too.

Note: Lanfen means fragrant flower or Orchid in English

NATURE

PREDESTINED

Sunlight shoots the space from Hooton Roberts
to Gormire Lake, mornings geyser up with clouds,
and winter, passing into shadows,
waves quickly then deserts you. Forsythia
loses its bright yellow, and small birds
coming back pass swiftly into spring
as buds on rhododendrons open.
Bees swarm, butterflies mate, and winter
no longer invents you, and where the day goes
you follow past hedgerow and furrow,
on sidewalks flowing over with chatter,
an evanescent child in this sunlit hive,
in the ever-widening blast, conceiving
your story like the flower conceives its fruit.

SPRING

The mildest April in years is turned soil
no longer dreaming of sunlight, fallow ground,
seeding set in furrows as sun and soft rain
leave nothing to chance, and the land succumbs
to old habits, yet takes us by surprise.

The interruption breaks up the monotony
of the landscape that fulfills its promise,
the allegiance of plants to certain fields,
the invasion of roots and weeds mingled with
shadows and light beyond the grey picket fence
where we, having nowhere to go but here,
wander the green fields for a while.

SEED

By the lane to Viner's pond, there are sparrows
and robins, a hedge of nests in a valley

of unsettled fog, there are horsetail reeds,
blue iris, and sweet flag where you jump

the still water with smooth stones, as sparrows
scatter into horizons like saints that send

out their light until nothing can hide
but the secret lives of flowers and plants,

their petals reaching toward the sun
in blind determination and patterns of past

generations, that survive by dropping
their seed into this source of minutes and bees.

MEMORY

What we come from has too many rivers,
exaggerated terrains, talk that never
took place, hours in sunlight we kept
and call memories, changes we wrought in them
so we could say we lived, laughed, cried,
and it meant something. Even the true story
is ingeniously made: a girl with wings
is in it, honey bees are swarming,
and love, the little dog Toby, goes out
the door and up the hill, and when
the story ends, there is still time for silence
and awe as we wait at the bottom
of the lane for God to appear, and when
He doesn't, there are no recriminations.

ECHO

In my echo days, days of the loud shout,
over meadow, moss, rocks, and fallen
trees, I raged like a blast of fire through the fern.
I was a chased fox, a red buck deer,
racing on through my boyhood years.
I was wilder then, without awareness, when—
drowning my shy self in green
and disturbing a thousand lives
in cobweb woods—it came in the winter
of my youngest years, a black dot
out of the white horizon's glare, and I,
in the naked uplands among the splashing fern,
suddenly looked up and stared
at the rent in the whiteness of my years.

BERRIES

We amble up to High Melton, buckets
swinging by our sides, the morning streaming
up with birds and clouds, the sky so close we
can almost touch it. The fields are green oceans
below us, the people brush marks, and we,
eager as puppies, rush into the thicket,
cutting our hands and fingers, filling
the empty buckets. All-day the sweetness
won't stop. Here we will never die, never
grow old and never be sick, and in these moments
our story is a happy one. Looking up,
everything is where it should be; the berries
are plump and ready, and nothing's
in the way of becoming wiser too late.

LIZA

SUNDAY

They stripped me, painted graffiti on my body,
and called me Bird; the big one with stringy blonde hair,

and *Sparrow* tattooed on his arm bit me--
his big calloused hands on my breasts, his fingers between my
legs.

I begged God to erase my body; my prayers were everywhere,
like crumpled notes on the floor, or birds bumping against
windows and doors,

trying to escape to that holy ear. The girl in black laughed,
and the silent one wrote, "Fuck me," on my back

with a bright red crayon. Sparrow raped me. Outside, the day
was where I left it in the leaves, and the children's voices, bees

looked in the window, the lights went on in the dogwoods, and
the air
was infused with the idea of rescue. Outside, I could hear the
evening

chugging along without me, and I hoped that God
was searching inside Sunday for my prayers.

When I escaped as if in a dream, my knife securing the silence,
Paul and Mother kept me alive. We fled to America.

INSIDE THE BUBBLE WITH LIZA

Everyone keeps cheering you on,
not to win, but to cross the street,

mow the lawn, and keep the driveway clean,
though the dramas you binge on

put you at odds with the suburban plot,
sometimes ending in grief,

yet those beliefs are pulling you
in a direction you want to believe in,

though it was never your choice, so
you play your part, imagining

you are here for a reason as your epic
contracts to a story

of less jealousy and aggrandizement
yet not tempered enough for you to fit in,

so the happy life is just guesswork
like the meaning of music?

And later when your grandiose stories,
as big as the center ring of a circus,

describe childhood, your wishful thinking
doesn't elude you, but inside and out

are different now, and what you give freely
is not yourself, but the idea of yourself.

DINNER

Liza was arguing with her brother, Paul.
Dinner was on the stove—shellfish and Spanish rice.

He was laughing at her opinions, picked up
his harmonica, and blew into it as loud as he could
before she answered his taunt with her own.

Liza looked at the boiling water as Nola, the dog,
scampered out of the room, and I inched toward the door,
but Liza smiled and put Paul's and my dinner on plates.

I sat down by the window and was laughing at Paul
waltzing around the kitchen with his happy harmonica,

touching Liza on the head as he passed her,
touching the walls, the ceiling, and the chandelier,
touching Nola as she returned to Liza's legs.

Liza, still smiling, walked to the table and said
in her most polite voice while looking at Paul,
"Dinner is served," and threw the plates out the window.

DEAD MAN

Yesterday, Liza held a shotgun to my head,
and would have pulled the trigger, but

she did not want to leave her son an orphan.
Now I'm taking up dancing to bring us together.

"Is that wise?" Is the only advice I get,
and later when she carries her shotgun

like a third leg, I know dancing with a broom
is safer, so I'm walking away from a dead man

with my name, taking up residence in this green world,
leaving my end inside Liza's scheming head,

traveling toward the horizon—my clothes
in a duffle bag. Liza is far away,

cleaning her weapon, and I am a man again
making my way across America.

LIZA SPEAKS

"I don't know what to feel when listening
to babies cry, or when I'm thinking

of a man's name, or watching water
as light strikes its surface. My brain

does not see the pain of others or the joy,
too much was taken from me

by those who said they loved me, yet loved
themselves better. I try to see without mirrors

beyond my brain's chatter or the opinions
of others but through the eyes of my son, Saul,

his existence awakens my own.
Sometimes I think I'm becoming God."

PEAK EXPERIENCE

I'm watching Saul and Liza's first husband, Sam,
go down the stairs of our house to his car.

Liza says, to my surprise, I hate Sam;
the steps are icy; I hope he breaks his neck.

When she takes me off the pedestal my name is, You.
Don't do this, I say. You have played with my emotions,

so be quiet, she says, your words sound like weapons,
your daughter's a Nazi, your son a devil worshipper.

Self-aggrandizement, she continues, determines your destiny
as you blindly count on your future to solve everything

and fall from the small amount of grace allotted you by being
yourself.
Your life is an accident you want to erect monuments to

as if in you is something significant and fine. Your delusions
keep you innocent, hiding the black hole that is your fate.

I see her subjective reality has doors and windows
and a landscape populated by threatening strangers,

but fucking is intense, and she and I do it day and night.
She will kill me, but I can't leave until she does.

My psychiatrist says I'm having a peak experience.
I tell him Liza is a pathological liar. He says he envies me.

ABORTIONS

You are the echo of their deaths,
for a moment, they made your life
exemplary and maybe immortal.

Tell them you were born for better work
or do not believe in them.

Study forgetting in your library of lies,
and tell the air it is you who are real,

slouching into exile; it is you who
will not be blamed for giving too many answers

to the same question; it is you who
refuse to see the light coming out of what is.

Tell them they were intruders,
having no rights in these matters,
struck from behind by their mother.

BANSHEE

Robbed and menaced
at gunpoint in our house
with only her guile
to protect her, who
threw boiling water
in the face of one
intruder, turning Nola,
the dog, on the other,

and made the whole thing up
to justify buying
a shotgun she uses
to kill me. Don't
forget my shadow
running down the hall
in front of me. Don't
forget to turn when I do,

my shadow patiently
waiting for me to join it
on the floor after she
blows my brains out
and later falls on my coffin
with a wail like a Banshee
in such grief, I think
she'll join me

with a plate of shellfish
and Spanish rice,
and a torch to pass
through the dirt and stones
into the airless night
to listen to silence,
but Liza goes the other way
babbling she loves me.

PAUSE

I wanted to die, give up
the Peloton, the vitamin C,

ready to jump when
the subway arrived,

or take one desperate
swallow of lye, or contract

a sudden disease
that would end me midway.

Now I'm taking a pause,
not ready to live,

not ready to die,
knowing isolation is sweet

as happiness seeps in
when I'm with my little dog,

Pete, who pacifies me
when ambition, craziness,

and greed once pushed
me out the door.

Now money schemes
are cast aside to make

room for doing nothing.
After all this freedom

beckons me to be myself
when drawn into the music

of Ravel now playing
as if into reality

since my only purpose
is to be and nothing else.

I want time for what is
outside of me, to wander

through fields of wild grass,
fern, and milkweed,

to watch the twilight turn
the land into strips of gold,

never to return to the country
of blows and kicks

where the future waits
like a cockroach behind a wall.

REVENGE

After Liza blows my brains out,
all my thoughts and skills

scatter like pigeons,
even my senses flutter away.

Fifty years of days and nights
walk out the door in a parade.

I can hear the sounds of wings
as each of my words becomes a departure.

My wishes are dead bees,
and my voices are cats seeking an exit.

I can see Liza bent over me,
poking around until she finds

our last argument bunched up
at the side of my head like a dead mouse.

Her face looms over me
with the curiosity of a fox.

I look straight up at her
and say, "There is evidence,"

but she doesn't hear me,
and ponders whether to call

the police, or have a cup
of coffee with a sweet bun.

After Liza buries me, I listen
to the greening of plants, to my

body become the land before its time,
to my children's voices,

like the light in maple trees,
and all I can think of

is one word remaining
on my vanishing tongue,

a word worrying Liza
when she walks into town,

looking behind or looking up,
expecting me to fall on her head

from God's Hands, wondering
how to kill me a second time.

ABOUT THE AUTHOR

Keith Keenan

 Keith Keenan was born in Manhattan. When he was 8, his mother took him, and his two brothers to live in her hometown in the North of England. When he returned to New York City at 18, he held many jobs. In one of them he learned to program computers, and started a company that years later, he sold, giving him time to write

www.ingramcontent.com/pod-product-compliance
Lightning Source LLC
Chambersburg PA
CBHW070804200626
46811CB00023B/1601